Lettice

The Ice Princess

Mandy Stanley

HarperCollins *Children's Books*

Lettice Rabbit and her family lived high up on top of the hill. Nibble, nibble, hop, hop, every day was the same, until one winter afternoon...

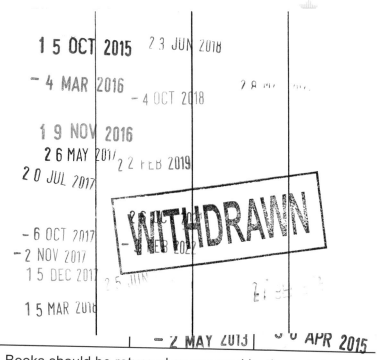

To Sue Buswell, for giving me a tiny pair
of skating boots... just the right size for Lettice x

www.mandystanley.com

First published in paperback in Great Britain by HarperCollins Children's Books in 2011

1 3 5 7 9 10 8 6 4 2

ISBN: 978-0-00-718404-0

HarperCollins Children's Books is a division of HarperCollins Publishers Ltd.

Visit our website at: www.harpercollins.co.uk

Printed in China

Lettice peeped out to find the trees garlanded with icicles. Down on the frozen lake children were whizzing over the ice on skates.

'That looks fun!' laughed Lettice, racing down to watch them.

Lettice leaned forwards further, and further...

but the snowy bank gave way...

and she slid out across the lake.

'There's a rabbit!' cried a voice.

Lettice twizzled round and fell flat on her nose
in front of a little girl.

'Hello!' said the little girl. 'My name's Ella.'

Ella's friends giggled as
Lettice tried to stand up...

wobbled about...

and landed on her bottom.

'We're having our own Winter Festival,'
explained the children. 'You can join in!'

'I wish I could,' whispered Lettice.
'But I haven't got anything to wear.'

'Don't worry!' said Ella. 'We'll help you dress up.'
She smiled at Lettice. 'I'm a bit nervous, too. You see,
I'm going to be crowned the Ice Princess! I'm sure
you're going to bring me luck.'

Ella helped Lettice skate over
to a big box full of dresses.

Lettice couldn't wait to try one on.

But they were all far, far too big.

So Ella said, 'Let's make a dress out of these scarves.'

There was a soft pink
one with pom-poms...

and a gold one covered
with sparkles.

Lettice wrapped them around herself.

She could hardly believe what a pretty
dress they made as she looked at her
reflection in the ice.

'Oooh! There's one thing we've forgotten,' said Ella's friend. 'Lettice hasn't got any skates!'

Lettice's face fell. How could she skate on her bare paws?

But the smallest girl said shyly, 'My lucky mascot is a tiny pair of skates and they look just the right size!'

Shivering with excitement, Lettice tried them on...

and they fitted perfectly!

At last it was time for the Festival to start.
The music was playing and Ella began to dance.
She was so graceful! Her friends joined in and
gently they tugged Lettice after them.

Ella's friend proudly carried the
shining tiara to crown the Ice Princess.

But all of a sudden, she skated
over a lump of ice and slipped!

Everyone shrieked in horror as
the tiara flew through the air...

and rolled towards the bank.
Lettice didn't stop to think.
Like a flash she was off,
whizzing over the ice.

The glittering tiara had
disappeared into the bushes
but in no time Lettice was
there, burrowing through
the snow!

The children whooped with joy as Lettice reappeared, snowy but triumphant.

Ella couldn't stop beaming with happiness as she was crowned the Ice Princess.

She took off her bracelet of silver stars and slipped it over Lettice's ears, saying, 'Now you're a princess, too!'

Then Lettice danced, all by herself, in front of the Ice Princess. It was growing darker and her starry crown twinkled in the lights of the coloured lanterns as she leaped and swayed to the music.

Soon it was time for the children to go home and they said Lettice could borrow the lucky skates to show her family.

'But you can keep my bracelet *for ever,*' said Ella, hugging her.

Lettice was still in a whirl when she got home.

'Come outside!' she cried.

Her little sisters and brothers peeped out and were very excited. 'Lettice is all starry, like a princess,' they giggled.

The moon shone large and silver over the lake as the rabbits raced down to play on the ice.

'I'm the luckiest rabbit alive,' sighed Lettice, and she showed them the dance of the Ice Princess.

Lettice

More dreams come true for
Lettice Rabbit in these
adorable picture books!

Lettice – The Dancing Rabbit
PB: 978-0-00-664777-5

Lettice – The Bridesmaid
PB: 978-0-00-718407-1

Lettice – The Fairy Ball
PB: 978-0-00-720195-2

Lettice – A Christmas Wish
PB: 978-0-00-716585-8

Lettice – The Flying Rabbit
PB: 978-0-00-714197-5